THE DARK DOOR

THE DARK DOOR

by Alan E. Nourse

1

It was almost dark when he awoke, and lay on the bed, motionless and trembling, his heart sinking in the knowledge that he should never have slept. For almost half a minute, eyes wide with fear, he lay in the silence of the gloomy room, straining to hear some sound, some indication of their presence.

But the only sound was the barely audible hum of his wrist watch and the dismal splatter of raindrops on the cobbled street outside. There was no sound to feed his fear, yet he knew then, without a flicker of doubt, that they were going to kill him.

He shook his head, trying to clear the sleep from his brain as he turned the idea over and over in his mind. He wondered why he hadn't realized it before, long before, back when they had first started this horrible, nerve-wracking cat-and-mouse game. The idea just hadn't occurred to him. But he knew the game-playing was over. They wanted to kill him now. And he knew that ultimately they *would* kill him. There was no way for him to escape.

He sat up on the edge of the bed, painfully, perspiration standing out on his bare back, and he waited, listening. How could he have slept, exposing himself so helplessly? Every ounce of his energy, all the skill and wit and shrewdness at his command were necessary in this cruel hunt; yet he had taken the incredibly terrible chance of sleeping, of losing consciousness, leaving himself wide open and helpless against the attack which he knew was inevitable.

How much had he lost? How close had they come while he slept?

Fearfully, he walked to the window, peered out, and felt his muscles relax a little. The gray, foggy streets were still light. He still had a little time before the terrible night began.

He stumbled across the small, old-fashioned room, sensing that action of some sort was desperately needed. The bathroom was tiny; he stared in the battered, stained reflector unit, shocked at the red-eyed stubble-faced apparition that stared back at him.

This is Harry Scott, he thought, thirty-two years old, and in the prime of life, but not the same Harry Scott who started out on a ridiculous quest so many months ago. This Harry Scott was being hunted like an animal, driven by fear, helpless, and sure to die, unless he could find an escape, somehow. But there were too many of them for him to escape, and they were too clever, and they *knew* he knew too much.

He stepped into the shower-shave unit, trying to relax, to collect his racing thoughts. Above all, he tried to stay the fear that burned through his mind, driving him to panic and desperation. The memory of the last hellish night was too stark to allow relaxation—the growing fear, the silent, desperate hunt through the night; the realization that their numbers were increasing; his frantic search for a hiding place in the New City; and finally his panic-stricken, pell-mell flight down into the alleys and cobbled streets and crumbling frame buildings of the Old City.... Even more horrible, the friends who had turned on him, who turned out to be *like* them.

Back in the bedroom, he lay down again, his body still tense. There were sounds in the building, footsteps moving around on the floor overhead, a door banging somewhere. With every sound, every breath of noise, his muscles tightened still further, freezing him in fear. His own breath was shallow and rapid in his ears as he lay, listening, waiting.

If only something would happen! He wanted to scream, to bang his head against the wall, to run about the room smashing his fist into doors, breaking every piece of furniture. It was the *waiting*, the eternal waiting, and running, waiting some more, feeling the net drawing tighter and tighter as he waited, feeling the measured, unhurried tread behind him, always following, coming closer and closer, as though he were a mouse on a string, twisting and jerking helplessly.

If only they would move, do something he could counter.

But he wasn't even sure any more that he could detect them. And they were so careful never to move into the open.

5

THE DARK DOOR

He jumped up feverishly, moved to the window, and peered between the slats of the dusty, old-fashioned blind at the street below.

An empty street at first, wet, gloomy. He saw no one. Then he caught the flicker of light in an entry several doors down and across the street, as a dark figure sparked a cigarette to life. Harry felt the chill run down his back again. Still there, then, still waiting, a hidden figure, always present, always waiting....

Harry's eyes scanned the rest of the street rapidly. Two three-wheelers rumbled by, their rubber hissing on the wet pavement. One of them carried the blue-and-white of the Old City police, but the car didn't slow up or hesitate as it passed the dark figure in the doorway. They would never help me anyway, Harry thought bitterly. He had tried that before, and met with ridicule and threats. There would be no help from the police in the Old City.

Another figure came around a corner. There was something vaguely familiar about the tall body and broad shoulders as the man walked across the wet street, something Harry faintly recognized from somewhere during the spinning madness of the past few weeks.

The man's eyes turned up toward the window for the briefest instant, then returned steadfastly to the street. Oh, they were sly! You could never spot them looking at you, never for *sure*, but they were always there, always nearby. And there was no one he could trust any longer, no one to whom he could turn.

Not even George Webber.

Swiftly his mind reconsidered that possibility as he watched the figure move down the street. True, Dr. Webber had started him out on this search in the first place. But even Webber would never believe what he had found. Webber was a scientist, a researcher.

What could he do—go to Webber and tell him that there were men alive in the world who were *not* men, who were somehow men and something more?

6

Could he walk into Dr. Webber's office in the Hoffman Medical Center, walk through the gleaming bright corridors, past the shining metallic doors, and tell Dr. Webber that he had found people alive in the world who could actually see in four dimensions, live in four dimensions, *think* in four dimensions?

Could he explain to Dr. Webber that he knew this simply because in some way he had sensed them, and traced them, and discovered them; that he had not one iota of proof, except that he was being followed by them, hunted by them, even now, in a room in the Old City, waiting for them to strike him down?

He shook his head, almost sobbing. That was what was so horrible. He couldn't tell Webber, because Webber would be certain that he had gone mad, just like the rest. He couldn't tell anyone, he couldn't do anything. He could just wait, and run, and wait—

It was almost dark now and the creaking of the old board house intensified the fear that tore at Harry Scott's mind. Tonight was the night; he was sure of it. Maybe he had been foolish in coming here to the slum area, where the buildings were relatively unguarded, where anybody could come and go as he pleased. But the New City had hardly been safer, even in the swankiest private chamber in the highest building. They had had agents there, too, hunting him, driving home the bitter lesson of fear they had to teach him. Now he was afraid enough; now they were ready to kill him.

Down below he heard a door bang, and he froze, his back against the wall. There were footsteps, quiet voices, barely audible. His whole body shook and his eyes slid around to the window. The figure in the doorway still waited—but the other figure was not visible. He heard the steps on the stair, ascending slowly, steadily, a tread that paced itself with the powerful throbbing of his own pulse.

Then the telephone screamed out—

Harry gasped. The footsteps were on the floor below, moving steadily upward. The telephone rang again and again; the shrill jangling filled the room insistently. He waited until he couldn't wait

7

any longer. His hand fumbled in a pocket and leveled a tiny, dull-gray metal object at the door. With the other hand, he took the receiver from the hook.

"Harry! Is that you?"

His throat was like sandpaper and the words came out in a rasp. "What is it?"

"Harry, this is George—George Webber."

His eyes were glued to the door. "All right. What do you want?"

"You've got to come talk to us, Harry. We've been waiting for weeks now. You promised us. We've *got* to talk to you."

Harry still watched the door, but his breath came easier. The footsteps moved with ridiculous slowness up the stairs, down the hall toward the room.

"What do you want me to do? They've come to kill me."

There was a long pause. "Harry, are you sure?"

"Dead sure."

"Can you make a break for it?"

Harry blinked. "I could try. But it won't do any good."

"Well, at least try, Harry. Get here to the Hoffman Center. We'll help you all we can."

"I'll try." Harry's words were hardly audible as he set the receiver down with a trembling hand.

The room was silent. The footsteps had stopped. A wave of panic passed up Harry's spine; he crossed the room, threw open the door, stared up and down the hall, unbelieving.

The hall was empty. He started down toward the stairs at a dead run, and then, too late, saw the faint golden glow of a Parkinson Field across the dingy corridor. He gasped in fear, and screamed out once as he struck it.

And then, for seconds stretching into hours, he heard his scream echoing and re-echoing down long, bitter miles of hollow corridor.

2

George Webber leaned back in the soft chair, turning a quizzical glance toward the younger man across the room. He lit a long black cigar.

"Well?" His heavy voice boomed out in the small room. "Now that we've got him here, what do you think?"

The younger man glanced uncomfortably through the glass wall panel into the small dark room beyond. In the dimness, he could barely make out the still form on the bed, grotesque with the electrode-vernier apparatus already in place at its temples. Dr. Manelli looked away sharply, and leafed through the thick sheaf of chart papers in his hand.

"I don't know," he said dully. "I just don't know what to think."

The other man's laugh seemed to rise from the depths of his huge chest. His heavy face creased into a thousand wrinkles. Dr. Webber was a large man, his broad shoulders carrying a suggestion of immense power that matched the intensity of his dark, wide-set eyes. He watched Dr. Manelli's discomfort grow, saw the younger doctor's ears grow red, and the almost cruel lines in his face were masked as he laughed still louder.

"Trouble with you, Frank, you just don't have the courage of your convictions."

"Well, I don't see anything so funny about it!" Manelli's eyes were angry. "The man has a suspicious syndrome—so you've followed him, and spied on him for weeks on end, which isn't exactly highest ethical practice in collecting a history. I still can't see how you're justified."

Dr. Webber snorted, tossing his cigar down on the desk with disgust. "The man is insane. That's my justification. He's out of touch with reality. He's wandered into a wild, impossible, fantastic dream world. And we've got to get him out of it, because what he knows, what he's trying to hide from us, is so incredibly dangerous that we don't dare let him go."

THE DARK DOOR

The big man stared at Manelli, his dark eyes flashing. "Can't you see that? Or would you rather sit back and let Harry Scott go the way that Paulus and Wineberg and the others went?"

"But to use the Parkinson Field on him—" Dr. Manelli shook his head hopelessly. "He'd offered to come over, George. We didn't need to use it."

"Sure, he offered to come—fine, fine. But supposing he changed his mind on the way? For all we know, he had us figured into his paranoia, too, and never would have come near the Hoffman Center."

Dr. Webber shook his head. "We're not playing a game any more, Frank. Get that straight. I thought it was a game a couple of years ago, when we first started. But it ceased to be a game when men like Paulus and Wineberg walked in sane, healthy men, and came out blubbering idiots. That's no game any more. We're onto something big. And, if Harry Scott can lead us to the core of it, then I can't care too much what happens to Harry Scott."

Dr. Manelli stood up sharply, walked to the window, and looked down over the bright, clean buildings of the Hoffman Medical Center. Out across the terraced park that surrounded the glassed towers and shining metal of the Center rose the New City, tier upon tier of smooth, functional architecture, a city of dreams built up painfully out of the rubble of the older, ruined city.

"You could kill him," the young man said finally. "The psycho-integrator isn't any standard interrogative technique; it's dangerous and treacherous. You never know for sure just what you're doing when you dig down into a man's brain tissue with those little electrode probes."

"But we can learn the truth about Harry Scott," Dr. Webber broke in. "Six months ago, Harry Scott was working with us, a quiet, affable, pleasant young fellow, extremely intelligent, intensely co-operative. He was just the man we needed to work with us, an engineer who could take our data and case histories, study them, and subject them to a completely nonmedical analysis. Oh, we had to have it done—the problem's been with us for a hundred years now, growing ever since the 1950s and 60s—insanity in the population, growing, spreading without rhyme or reason, insinuating itself into every nook and cranny of our civilized life."

The big man blinked at Manelli. "Harry Scott was the new approach. We were too close to the problem. We needed a nonmedical outsider to take a look, to tell us what we were missing. So Harry Scott walked into the problem, and then abruptly lost contact with us. We finally track him down and find him gone, out of touch with reality, on the same wretched road that all the others went. With Harry, it's paranoia. He's being persecuted; he has the whole world against him, but most important—the factor we don't dare overlook—*he's no longer working on the problem*."

Manelli shifted uneasily. "I suppose that's right."

"Of course it's right!" Dr. Webber's eyes flashed. "Harry found something in those statistics. Something about the data, or the case histories; or something Harry Scott himself dug up opened a door for him to go through, a door that none of us ever dreamed existed. We don't know what he found on the other side of that door. Oh, we know what he *thinks* he found, all this garbage about people that look normal but walk through walls when nobody's looking, who think around corners instead of in straight-line logic. But what he *really* found there, we don't have any way of telling. We just know that whatever he *really* found is something new, something unsuspected; something so dangerous it can drive an intelligent man into the wildest delusions of paranoid persecution."

A new light appeared in Dr. Manelli's eyes as he faced the other doctor. "Wait a minute," he said softly. "The integrator is an *experimental* instrument, too."

Dr. Webber smiled slyly. "Now you're beginning to think," he said.

"But you'll see only what Scott himself believes. And *he* thinks his story is true."

"Then we'll have to break his story."

"*Break* it?"

"Certainly. For some reason, this delusion of persecution is far safer for Harry Scott than facing what he really found out. What we've got to do is to make this delusion *less* safe than the truth."

The room was silent for a long moment. Manelli looked up, his fingers trembling. "Let's hear it."

"It's very simple. Up to now, Harry Scott has had *delusions* of persecution. But now we're *really* going to persecute Harry Scott, as he's never been persecuted before."

3

At first he thought he was at the bottom of a deep well and he lay quite still, his eyes clamped shut, wondering where he was and how he could possibly have gotten there. He could feel the dampness and chill of the stone floor under him, and nearby he heard the damp, insistent drip of water splashing against stone. He felt his muscles tighten as the dripping sound forced itself against his senses. Then he opened his eyes.

His first impulse was to scream out wildly in unreasoning, suffocating fear. He fought it down, struggling to sit up in the blackness, his whole mind turned in bitter, hopeless hatred at the ones who had hunted him for so long, and now had trapped him.

Why?

Why did they torture him? Why not kill him outright, have done with it? He shuddered, and struggled to his feet, staring about him in horror.

It was not a well, but a small room, circular, with little rivulets of stale water running down the granite walls. The ceiling closed low over his head, and the only source of light came from the single doorway opening into a long, low stone passageway.

Wave after wave of panic rose in Harry's throat. Each time he fought down the urge to scream, to lie down on the ground and cover his face with his hands and scream in helpless fear. How could they have known the horror that lay in his own mind, the horror of darkness, of damp slimy walls and scurrying rodents, of the clinging, stale humidity of dungeon passageways? He himself had seldom recalled it, except in his most hideous dreams, yet he had known such fear as a boy, so many years ago, and now it was all around him. They had known somehow and *used it against him.*

Why?

He sank down on the floor, his head in his hands, trying to think straight, to find some clue in the turmoil bubbling through his mind that would tell him what had happened.

He had started down the hallway from his room, to find Dr. Webber and tell him about the other people—

He stopped short, looked up wide-eyed. *Had* he been going to Dr. Webber? Had he actually decided to go? Perhaps—yes, perhaps he had, though Webber would only laugh at such a ridiculous story. But the not-men who had hunted him would not laugh; to them, it would not be funny. They knew that it was true. And they knew he knew it was true.

But why not kill him? Why this torture? Why this horrible persecution that dug into the depths of his own nightmares to haunt him?

His breath came fast and a chilly sweat broke out on his forehead. *Where* was he? Was this some long forgotten vault in the depths of the Old City? Or was this another place, another world, perhaps, that the not-men, with their impossible powers, had created to torture him?

His eyes sought the end of the hall, saw the turn at the end, saw the light which seemed to come from the end; and then in an instant he was running down the damp passageway, his pulse pounding at his temples, until he could hardly gasp enough breath as he ran. Finally he reached the turn in the corridor where the light was brighter, and he swung around to stare at the source of the light, a huge, burning, smoky torch which hung from the wall.

Even as he looked at it, the torch went out, shutting him into inky blackness. The only sound at first was the desperation of his own breath; then he heard little scurrying sounds around his feet, and screamed involuntarily as something sleek and four-footed jumped at his chest with snapping jaws.

Shuddering, he fought the thing off, his fingers closing on wiry fur as he caught and squeezed. The thing went limp, and suddenly melted in his hands. He heard it splash as it struck the damp ground at his feet.

What were they doing to his mind?

He screamed out in horror, and followed the echoes of his own scream as he ran down the stone corridor, blindly, slipping on the wet stone floor, falling on his knees into inches of brackish water, scraping back to his feet with an uncontrollable convulsion of fear and loathing, only to run more—

The corridor suddenly broke into two and he stopped short. He didn't know how far, or how long, he had run, but it suddenly occurred to him that he was still alive, still safe. Only his mind was under attack, only his mind was afraid, teetering on the edge of control. And this maze of dungeon tunnels—where could such a thing exist, so perfectly outfitted to horrify him, so neatly fitting into his own pattern of childhood fears and terrors; from where could such a *very individual* attack on his sanity have sprung? From nowhere except....

Except from his own mind!

For an instant, he saw a flicker of light, thought he grasped the edge of a concept previously obscure to him. He stared around him, at the mist swirling down the damp, dark corridor, and thought of the rat that had melted in his hand. Suddenly, his mind was afire, searching through his experience with the strange not-men he had learned to detect, trying to remember everything he had learned and deduced about them before they began their brutal persecution.

They were men, and they looked like men, but they were different. They had other properties of mind, other capabilities that men did not have.

They were not-men. They could exist, and co-exist, two people in one frame, one person known, realized by all who saw, the other one concealed except from those who learned how to look. They could use their minds; they could rationalize correctly; they could use their curious four-dimensional knowledge to bring them to answers no three-dimensional man could reach.

But they couldn't project into men's minds!

Carefully, Harry peered down the misty tunnels. They were clever, these creatures, and powerful. Since they had discovered that he knew them, they had done their work of fear and terror on his mind skillfully. But they were limited, too; they couldn't make things happen that were not true—fantasies, illusions....

Yes, this dungeon was an illusion. It *had* to be.

He cursed and started down the right-hand corridor, his heart sinking. There was no such place and he knew it. He was walking in a dream, a fantasy that had no substance, that could do no more than frighten him, drive him insane; yet he must already have lost his mind to be accepting such an illusion.

Why had he delayed? Why hadn't he gone to the Hoffman Center, laid the whole story before Dr. Webber and Dr. Manelli at the very first, told them what he had found? True, they might have thought him insane, but they wouldn't have put him to torture. They might even have believed him enough to investigate what he told them, and then the cat would have been out of the bag. The tale would have been incredible, but at least his mind would have been safe.

He turned down another corridor and walked suddenly into waist-deep water, so cold it numbed his legs. He stopped again to force back the tendrils of unreasoning horror that brushed his mind.

THE DARK DOOR

Nothing could really harm him. He would merely wait until his mind finally reached a balance again. There might be no end; it might be a ghastly trap, but he would wait.

Strangely, the mist was becoming greenish in color as it swirled toward him in the damp vaulted passageway. His eyes began watering a little and the lining of his nose started to burn. He stopped short, newly alarmed, and stared at the walls, rubbing the tears away to clear his vision. The greenish-yellow haze grew thicker, catching his eyes and burning like a thousand furies, ripping into his throat until he was choking and coughing, as though great knives sliced through his lungs.

He tried to scream, and started running, blindly. Each gasping breath was an agony as the blistering gas dug deeper and deeper into his lungs. Reason departed from him; he was screaming incoherently as he stumbled up a stony ramp, crashed into a wall, spun around and smashed blindly into another. Then something caught at his shirt.

He felt the heavy planks and pounded iron scrollwork of a huge door, and threw himself upon it, wrenching at the old latch until the door swung open with a screech of rusty hinges. He fell forward on his face, and the door swung shut behind him.

He lay face down, panting and sobbing in the stillness.

Coarse hands grasped his collar, jerking him rudely to his feet, and he opened his eyes. Across the dim, vaulted room he could see the shadowy form of a man, a big man, with a broad chest and powerful shoulders, a man whose rich voice Harry almost recognized, but whose face was deep in shadow. As Harry wiped the tears from his tortured eyes, he heard the man's voice rumble out at him:

"Perhaps you've had enough now to change your mind about telling us the truth."

Harry stared, not quite comprehending. "The—the truth?"

The man's voice was harsh, cutting across the room impatiently. "The truth, I said. The problem, you fool, what you saw, what you learned; you know perfectly well what I'm referring to. But we'll

16

swallow no more of this silly four-dimensional superman tale, so don't bother to start it."

"I—I don't understand you. It's—it's true—" Again he tried to peer across the room. "Why are you hunting me like this? What are you trying to do to me?"

"We want the truth. We want to know what you saw."

"But—but *you're* what I saw. You know what I found out. I mean—" He stopped, his face going white. His hand went to his mouth, and he stared still harder. "Who are you?" he whispered.

"The truth!" the man roared. "You'd better be quick, or you'll be back in the corridor."

"*Webber!*"

"Your last chance, Harry."

Without warning, Harry was across the room, flying across the desk, crashing into the big man's chest. With a scream of fury he fought, driving his fists into the powerful chest, wrenching at the thick, flailing arms of the startled man.

"*It's you!*" he screamed. "It's you that's been torturing me. It's you that's been hunting me down all this time, not the other people, you and your crowd of ghouls have been at my throat!"

He threw the big man off balance, dropped heavily on him as he fell back to the ground, glared down into the other's angry brown eyes.

And then, as though he had never been there at all, the big man vanished, and Harry sat back on the floor, his whole body shaking with frustrated sobs as his mind twisted in anguish.

He had been wrong, completely wrong, ever since he had discovered the not-men. Because he had thought *they* had been the ones who hunted and tortured him for so long. And now he knew how far he had been wrong. For the face of the shadowy man, the man behind the nightmare he was living, was the face of Dr. George Webber.

*

17

"You're a fool," said Dr. Manelli sharply, as he turned away from the sleeping figure on the bed to face the older man. "Of all the ridiculous things, to let him connect you with this!" The young doctor turned abruptly and sank down in a chair, glowering at Dr. Webber. "You haven't gotten to first base yet, but you've just given Scott enough evidence to free himself from integrator control altogether, if he gives it any thought. But I suppose you realize that."

"Nonsense," Dr. Webber retorted. "He had enough information to do that when we first started. I'm no more worried now than I was then. I'm sure he doesn't know enough about the psycho-integrator to be able voluntarily to control the patient-operator relationship to any degree. Oh, no, he's safe enough. But you've missed the whole point of that little interview." Dr. Webber grinned at Manelli.

"I'm afraid I have. It looked to me like useless bravado."

"The persecution, man, the *persecution*! He's shifted his sights! Before that interview, the *not-men* were torturing him, remember? Because they were afraid he would report his findings to me, of course. But now it's *I* that's against him." The grin widened. "You see where that leads?"

"You're talking almost as though you believed this story about a different sort of people among us."

Dr. Webber shrugged. "Perhaps I do."

"Oh, come now, George."

Dr. Webber's eyebrows went up and the grin disappeared from his face.

"Harry Scott believes it, Frank. We mustn't forget that, or miss its significance. Before Harry started this investigation of his, he wouldn't have paid any attention to such nonsense. But he believes it now."

"But Harry Scott is insane. You said it yourself."

"Ah, yes," said Dr. Webber. "Insane. Just like the others who started to get somewhere along those lines of investigation. Try to analyze the growing incidence of insanity in the population and you yourself go insane. You've got to be crazy to be a psychiatrist. It's an old joke, but it isn't very funny any more. And it's too much for coincidence.

"And then consider the nature of the insanity—a full-blown paranoia—oh, it's amazing. A cunning organization of men who are *not*-men, a regular fairy story, all straight from Harry Scott's agile young mind. But now it's *we* who are persecuting him, *and he still believes his fairy tale.*"

"So?"

Dr. Webber's eyes flashed angrily. "It's too neat, Frank. It's clever, and it's powerful, whatever we've run up against. But I think we've got an ace in the hole. We have Harry Scott."

"And you really think he'll lead us somewhere?"

Dr. Webber laughed. "That door I spoke of that Harry peeked through, I think he'll go back to it again. I think he's started to open that door already. And this time I'm going to follow him through."

4

It seemed incredible, yet Harry Scott knew he had not been mistaken. It had been Dr. Webber's face he had seen, a face no one could forget, an unmistakable face. And that meant that it had been Dr. Webber who had been persecuting him.

But why? He had been going to report to Webber when he had run into that golden field in the rooming-house hallway. And suddenly things had changed.

Harry felt a chill reaching to his fingers and toes. Yes, something had changed, all right. The attack on him had suddenly become butcherous, cruel, sneaking into his mind somehow to use his most dreaded nightmares against him. There was no telling what new horrors might be waiting for him. But he knew that he would lose his mind unless he could find an escape.

He was on his feet, his heart pounding. He had to get out of here, wherever he was. He had to get back to town, back to the city, back to where people were. If he could find a place to hide, a place where he could rest, he could try to think his way out of this ridiculous maze, or at least try to understand it.

He wrenched at the door to the passageway, started through, and smashed face-up against a solid brick wall.

He cried out and jumped back from the wall. Blood trickled from his nose. The door was *walled up*, the mortar dry and hard.

Frantically, he glanced around the room. There were no other doors, only the row of tiny windows around the ceiling of the room, pale, ghostly squares of light.

He pulled the chair over to the windows, peered out through the cobwebbed openings to the corridor beyond.

It was not the same hallway as before, but an old, dirty building corridor, incredibly aged, with bricks sagging away from the walls. At the end he could see stairs, and even the faintest hint of sunlight coming from above.

Wildly, he tore at the masonry of the window, chipping away at the soggy mortar with his fingers until he could squeeze through the opening. He fell to the floor of the corridor outside.

It was much colder and the silence was no longer so intense. He seemed to feel, rather than hear, the surging power, the rumble of many machines, the little, almost palpable vibrations from far above him.

He started in a dead run down the musty corridor to the stairs and began to climb them, almost stumbling over himself in his eagerness.

After several flights, the brick walls gave way to cleaner plastic, and suddenly a brightly lighted corridor stretched before him.

Panting from the climb, Harry ran down the corridor to the end, wrenched open a door, and looked out anxiously.

He was almost stunned by the bright light. At first he couldn't orient himself as he stared down at the metal ramp, the moving strips of glowing metal carrying the throngs of people, sliding along the thoroughfare before him, unaware of him watching, unaware of any change from the usual. The towering buildings before him rose to unbelievable heights, bathed in ever-changing rainbow colors, and he felt his pulse thumping in his temples as he gaped.

He was in the New City, of that there was no doubt. This was the part of the great metropolis which had been built again since the devastating war that had nearly wiped the city from the Earth a decade before. These were the moving streets, the beautiful residential apartments, following the modern neo-functional patterns and participational design which had completely altered the pattern of city living. The Old City still remained, of course—the slums, the tenements, the skid-rows of the metropolis—but this was the teeming heart of the city, a new home for men to live in.

And this was the stronghold where the not-men could be found, too. The thought cut through Harry's mind, sending a tremor up his spine. He had found them here; he had uncovered his first clues here, and discovered them; and even now his mind was filled with the horrible, paralyzing fear he had felt that first night when he had made the discovery. Yet he knew now that he dared not go back where he had come from.

At least he could understand why the not-men might have feared and persecuted him, but he could not understand the horrible assault that Dr. Webber had unleashed. And somehow he found Dr. Webber's attack infinitely more frightening.

He seemed to be safe here, though, at least for the moment.

Quickly he moved down onto the nearest moving sidewalk heading toward the living section of the New City. He knew where he could go there, where he could lock himself in, a place where he could think, possibly find a way to fight off Dr. Webber's attack of nightmares.

He settled back on a bench on the moving sidewalk, watching the city slide past him for several minutes before he noticed the curious shadow-form which seemed to whisk out of his field of vision every time he looked.

THE DARK DOOR

They were following him again! He looked around wildly as the sidewalk moved swiftly through the cool evening air. Far above, he could see the shimmering, iridescent screen that still stood to protect the New City from the devastating virus attacks which might again strike down from the skies without warning. Far ahead he could see the magnificent "bridge" formed by the sidewalk crossing over to the apartment area, where the thousands who worked in the New City were returning to their homes.

Someone was still following him.

Presently he heard the sound, so close to his ear he jumped, yet so small he could hardly identify it as a human voice. "What was it you found, Harry? What did you discover? Better tell, better tell."

He saw the rift in the moving sidewalk coming, far ahead, a great, gaping rent in the metal fabric of the swiftly moving escalator, as if a huge blade were slicing it down the middle. Harry's hand went to his mouth, choking back a scream as the hole moved with incredible rapidity down the center of the strip, swallowing up whole rows of the seats, moving straight toward his own.

He glanced in fright over the side just as the sidewalk moved out onto the "bridge," and he gasped as he saw the towering canyons of buildings fall far below, saw the seats tumble end over end, heard the sounds of screaming blend into the roar of air by his ears.

Then the rift screamed by him with a demoniac whine and he sank back onto his bench, gasping as the two cloven halves of the strip clanged back together again.

He stared at the people around him on the strip and they stared back at him, mildly, unperturbed, and returned to their evening papers as the strip passed through the first local station on the other side of the "bridge."

Harry Scott sprang to his feet, moving swiftly across the slower strips for the exit channels. He noted the station stop vaguely, but his only thought now was speed, desperate speed, fear-driven speed to put into action the plan that had suddenly burst in his mind.

He knew that he had reached his limit. He had come to a point beyond which he couldn't fight alone.

Somehow, Webber had burrowed into his brain, laid his mind open to attacks of nightmare and madness that he could never hope to fight. Facing this alone, he would lose his mind. His only hope was to go for help to the ones he feared only slightly less, the ones who had minds capable of fighting back for him.

He crossed under the moveable sidewalks and boarded the one going back into the heart of the city. Somewhere there, he hoped, he would find the help he needed. Somewhere back in that city were men he had discovered who were men and something more.

*

Frank Manelli carefully took the blood pressure of the sleeping figure on the bed; then turned to the other man. "He'll be dead soon," he snapped. "Another few minutes now is all it'll take. Just a few more."

"Absurd. There's nothing in these stimuli that can kill him." George Webber sat tense, his eyes fixed on the pale fluctuating screen near the head of the bed.

"His own mind can kill him! He's on the run now; you've broken him loose from his nice safe paranoia. His mind is retreating, running back to some other delusions. It's escaping to the safety his fantasy people can afford him, these not-men he thinks about."

"Yes, yes," agreed Dr. Webber, his eyes eager. "Oh, he's on the run now."

"But what will he do when he finds there aren't any 'not-men' to save him? What will he do then?"

Webber looked up, frowning and grim. "Then we'll know what he found behind the dark door that he opened, that's what."

"No, you're wrong! He'll die. He'll find nothing and the shock will kill him. My God, Webber, you can't tamper with a man's mind like this and hope to save his life! You're obsessed; you've always been obsessed by this impossible search for something in our society, some undiscovered factor to account for the mental illness, the divergent minds, but you can't kill a man to trace it down!"

"It's too neat," said Webber. "He comes back to tell us the truth, and we call him insane. We say he's paranoid, throw him in restraint, place him in an asylum; and we never *know* what he found. The truth is too incredible; when we hear it, it must be insanity we're hearing."

The big doctor laughed, jabbing his thumb at the screen. "This isn't insanity we're seeing. Oh, no, this is the answer we're following. I won't stop now. I've waited too long for this show."

"Well, I say stop it while he's still alive."

Dr. Webber's eyes were deadly. "Get out, Frank," he said softly. "I'm not stopping now."

His eyes returned to the screen, to the bobbing figure that the psycho-integrator traced on the fluorescent background. Twenty years of search had led him here, and now he knew the end was at hand.

5

It was a wild, nightmarish journey. At every step, Harry's senses betrayed him: his wrist watch turned into a brilliant blue-green snake that snapped at his wrist; the air was full of snarling creatures that threatened him at every step. But he fought them off, knowing that they would harm him far less than panic would. He had no idea where to hunt, nor whom to try to reach, but he knew they were there in the New City, and somehow he knew they would help him, if only he could find them.

He got off the moving strip as soon as the lights of the center of the city were clear below, and stepped into the self-operated lift that sped down to ground level. From the elevator, he moved on to one of the long, honeycombed concourses, filled with passing shoppers who stared at the colorful, enticing three-dimensional displays.

At one of the intersections ahead, he spotted a visiphone station, and dropped onto the little seat before the screen. There had been a number, if only he could recall it. But as he started to dial, the silvery screen shattered into a thousand sparkling glass chips, showering the floor with crystal and sparks.

Harry cursed, grabbed the hand instrument, and jangled frantically for the operator. Before she could answer, the instrument grew warm in his hand, then hot and soft, like wax. Slowly, it melted and ran down his arm.

He bolted out into the stream of people, trying desperately to draw some comfort from the crowd around him.

He felt utterly alone; he *had* to contact the not-men who were in the city, warn them, before they spotted him, of the attack he carried with him. If he were leading his pursuer, he could expect no mercy from the ones whose help he sought. He knew the lengths to which they would go to remain undetected in the society around them. Yet he had to find them.

In the distance, he saw a figure waiting, back against one of the show windows. Harry stopped short, ducked into a doorway, and peered out fearfully. Their eyes locked for an instant; then the figure moved on. Harry felt a jolt of horror surge through him. Dr. Webber hunting him in person!

He ducked out of the doorway, turned and ran madly in the opposite direction, searching for an up escalator he could catch. Behind him he heard shots, heard the angry whine of bullets past his ear.

He breathed in great, gasping sobs as he found an almost empty escalator, and bounded up it four steps at a time. Below, he could see Webber coming too, his broad shoulders forcing their way relentlessly through the mill of people.

Panting, Harry reached the top, checked his location against a wall map, and started down the long ramp which led toward the building he had tried to call.

Another shot broke out behind him. The wall alongside powdered away, leaving a gaping hole. On impulse, he leaped into the hole, running through to the rear of the building as the weakened wall swayed and crumbled into a heap of rubble just as Webber reached the place Harry had entered.

Harry breathed a sigh of relief and raced up the stairs of the building to reach a ramp on another level. He turned his eyes toward the tall building at the end of the concourse. There he could hide and relax and try, somehow, to make a contact.

Someone fell into step beside him and took his arm gently but firmly. Harry jerked away, turning terrified eyes to the one who had joined him.

"Quiet," said the man, steering him over toward the edge of the concourse. "Not a sound. You'll be all right."

Harry felt a tremor pass through his mind, the barest touching of mental fingertips, a recognition that sent a surge of eager blood through his heart.

He stopped short, facing the man. "I'm being followed," he gasped. "You can't take me anywhere you don't want Webber to follow, or you'll be in terrible danger."

The stranger shrugged and smiled briefly. "You're not here. You're in a psycho-integrator. It can hurt you, if you let it. But it can't hurt me." He stepped up his pace slightly, and in a moment they turned abruptly into a darkened cul-de-sac.

Suddenly, they were moving *through* the wall of the building into the brilliantly lit lobby of the tall building. Harry gasped, but the stranger led him without a sound toward the elevator, stepped aboard with him, and sped upward, the silence broken only by the whish-whish-whish of the passing floors. Finally they stepped out into a quiet corridor and down through a small office door.

A man sat behind the desk in the office, his face quiet, his eyes very wide and dark. He hardly glanced at Harry, but turned his eyes to the other man.

"Set?" he asked.

"Couldn't miss now."

26

The man nodded and looked at last at Harry. "You're upset," he murmured. "What's bothering you?"

"Webber," said Harry hoarsely. "He's following me here. He'll spot you. I tried to warn you before I came, but I couldn't."

The man at the desk smiled. "Webber again, eh? Our old friend Webber. That's all right. Webber's at the end of his tether. There's nothing he can do to stop us. He's trying to attack with force, and he fails to realize that time and thought are on our side. The time when force would have succeeded against us is long past. But now there are many of us, almost as many as not."

Harry stared shrewdly at the man behind the desk. "Then why are you so afraid of Webber?" he asked.

"Afraid?"

"You know you are. Long ago you threatened me, if I reported to him. You watched me, played with me. Why are you afraid of him?"

The man sighed. "Webber is premature. We are stalling for time, that's all. We wait. We have grown from so very few, back in the 1940s and 50s, but the time for quiet usurpation of power has not quite arrived. But men like Webber force our hand, discover us, try to expose us."

Harry Scott's face was white, his hands shaking. "And what do you do to them?"

"We—deal with them."

"And those like me?"

The man smiled lopsidedly. "Those like Paulus and Wineberg and the rest—they're happy, really, like little children. But one like you is so much more useful." He pointed almost apologetically to the small screen on his desk.

Harry looked at it, realization dawning. He watched the huge, broad-shouldered figure moving down the hallway toward the door.

"Webber was dangerous to you?"

"Unbelievably dangerous. So dangerous we would use any means to trap him."

Suddenly the door burst open and there stood Webber, a triumphant Webber, face flushed, eyes wide, as he stared at the man behind the desk.

The man smiled back and said, "Come on in, George. We've been waiting for you."

Webber stepped through the door. "Manelli, you fool!"

There was a blinding flash as he crossed the threshold. A faint crackle of sound reached Harry's ears; then the world blacked out....

*

It might have been minutes, or hours, or days. The man who had been behind the desk was leaning over Harry, smiling down at him, gently bandaging the trephine wounds at his temples.

"Gently," he said, as Harry tried to sit up. "Don't try to move. You've been through a rough time."

Harry peered up at him. "You're—not Dr. Webber."

"No. I'm Dr. Manelli. Dr. Webber's been called away—an accident. He'll be some time recovering. I'll be taking care of you."

Vaguely, Harry was aware that something was peculiar, something not quite as it should be. The answer slowly dawned on him.

"The statistical analysis!" he exclaimed. "I was supposed to get some data from Dr. Webber about an analysis, something about rising insanity rates."

Dr. Manelli looked blank. "Insanity rates? You must be mistaken. You were brought here for an immunity examination, nothing more. But you can check with Dr. Webber, when he gets back."

6

George Webber sat in the little room, trembling, listening, his eyes wide in the thick, misty darkness. He knew it would be a matter of time now. He couldn't run much farther. He hadn't seen them, true. Oh, they had been very clever, but they thought they were dealing with a fool, and they weren't. He *knew* they'd been following him; he'd known it for a long time now.

It was just as he had been telling the man downstairs the night before: they were everywhere—your neighbor upstairs, the butcher on the corner, your own son or daughter, maybe even the man you were talking to—*everywhere*!

And of course he had to warn as many people as he possibly could before *they* caught him, throttled him off, as they had threatened to if he talked to anyone.

If only the people would *listen* to him when he told them how cleverly it was all planned, how it would only be a matter of months, maybe only weeks or days before the change would happen, and the world would be quietly, silently taken over by the *other* people, the different people who could walk through walls and think in impossibly complex channels. And no one would know the difference, because business would go on as usual.

He shivered, sinking down lower on the bed. If only people would listen to him—

It wouldn't be long now. He had heard the stealthy footsteps on the landing below his room some time ago. This was the night they had chosen to make good their threats, to choke off his dangerous voice once and for all. There were footsteps on the stairs now, growing louder.

Wildly he glanced around the room as the steps moved down the hall toward his door. He rushed to the window, threw up the sash and screamed hoarsely to the silent street below: "Look out! They're here, all around us! They're planning to take over! Look out! Look out!"

The door burst open and there were two men moving toward him, grim-faced, dressed in white; tall, strong men with sad faces and strong arms.

One was saying, "Better come quietly, mister. No need to wake up the whole town."

www.ingramcontent.com/pod-product-compliance
Lightning Source LLC
Chambersburg PA
CBHW050920120626
46552CB00004B/1680